John Ruskin

The Mystery of Life and its Arts

John Ruskin

The Mystery of Life and its Arts

Reprint of the original, first published in 1869.

1st Edition 2022 | ISBN: 978-3-37502-256-3

Verlag (Publisher): Salzwasser Verlag GmbH, Zeilweg 44, 60439 Frankfurt, Deutschland
Vertretungsberechtigt (Authorized to represent): E. Roepke, Zeilweg 44, 60439 Frankfurt, Deutschland
Druck (Print): Books on Demand GmbH, In de Tarpen 42, 22848 Norderstedt, Deutschland

THE

MYSTERY OF LIFE AND ITS ARTS.

THE

MYSTERY OF LIFE

AND

ITS ARTS.

BY

JOHN RUSKIN,

AUTHOR OF "MODERN PAINTERS," ETC.

NEW YORK:

JOHN WILEY & SON,

2 CLINTON HALL, ASTOR PLACE
1869.

THE MYSTERY OF LIFE AND ITS ARTS.

WHEN I accepted the privilege of addressing you to-day, I was not aware of a restriction with respect to the topics of discussion which may be brought before this Society—a restriction which, though entirely wise and right under the circumstances contemplated in its introduction, would necessarily have disabled me, thinking as I think, from preparing any lecture for you on the subject of art in a form which might be permanently useful. Pardon me, therefore, in so far as I must transgress such limitation; for indeed my infringement will be of the letter—not of the spirit—of your commands. In whatever I may say touching the religion which has been the foundation of art, or the policy which has contributed to its power, if I offend one, I shall offend all; for I shall take no note of any separations in creeds, or antagonisms in parties: neither do I fear that ultimately I shall offend any, by proving—or at least stating as capable of positive proof—the connection of all that is best in the crafts and arts of man, with the simplicity of his faith, and the sincerity of his patriotism.

But I speak to you under another disadvantage, by which I am checked in frankness of utterance, not here only, but everywhere; namely, that I am never fully aware how far my audiences are disposed to give me credit for real knowledge of my subject, or how far they grant me attention only because I have been sometimes thought an ingenious or pleasant essayist or speaker upon it. For I have had what, in many respects, I boldly call the misfortune, to set my words sometimes prettily together; not without a foolish vanity in the poor knack that I had of doing so, until I was heavily punished for this pride, by finding that many people thought of the words only, and cared nothing for their meaning. Happily, therefore, the power of using such pleasant language—if indeed it ever were mine—is passing away from me; and whatever I am now able to say at all, I find myself forced to say with great plainness. For my thoughts have changed also, as my words have; and whereas in earlier life, what little influence I obtained was due perhaps chiefly to the enthusiasm with which I was able to dwell on the beauty of the physical clouds, and of their colours in the sky; so all the influence I now desire to retain must be due to the earnestness with which I am endeavouring to trace the form and beauty of another kind of cloud than those; the bright cloud, of which it is written—

"What is your life? It is even as a vapour that appeareth for a little time, and then vanisheth away."

I suppose few people reach the middle or latter period of their age, without having at some moment of change or disappointment felt the truth of those bitter words; and been startled by the fading of the sunshine from the cloud of their life, into the sudden agony of the knowledge that the fabric of it was as fragile as a dream, and the endurance of it as transient as the dew. But it is not always that, even at such times of melancholy surprise, we can enter into any true perception that this human life shares, in the nature of it, not only the evanescence, but the mystery of the cloud; that its avenues are wreathed in darkness, and its forms and courses no less fantastic, than spectral and obscure; so that not only in the vanity which we cannot grasp, but in the shadow which we cannot pierce, it is true of this cloudy life of ours, that "man walketh in a vain shadow, and disquieteth himself in vain."

And least of all, whatever may have been the eagerness of our passions, or the height of our pride, are we able to understand in its depth the third and most solemn character in which our life is like those clouds of heaven; that to it belongs not only their transience, not only their mystery, but also their power; that in the cloud of the human soul there is a fire stronger than the lightning, and a grace more precious than the rain; and that though of the good and evil it shall one day be said alike, that the place that knew them knows them no more, there is an infinite separation between those whose brief presence had there been a blessing, like the mist of Eden that went up from the earth to water the garden, and those whose place knew them only as a drifting and changeful shade, of whom the heavenly sentence is, that they are "wells without water; clouds that are carried with a tempest, to whom the mist of darkness is reserved for ever."

To those among us, however, who have lived long enough to form some just estimate of the rate of the changes which are, hour by hour in accelerating catastrophe, manifesting themselves in the laws, the arts, and the creeds of men, it seems to me, that now at least, if never at any former time, the thoughts of the true nature of our life, and of its powers and responsibilities, should present themselves with absolute sadness and sternness. And although I know that this feeling is much deepened in my own mind by disappointment, which, by chance, has attended the greater number of my cherished purposes, I do not for that reason distrust the feeling itself, though I am on my guard against an exaggerated degree of it: nay, I rather believe that in periods of new effort and violent change, disappointment is a wholesome medicine; and that in the secret of it, as in the twilight so beloved by Titian, we may see the colours of things with deeper truth than in the most dazzling sunshine. And because these truths about the works of men, which I want to bring to-day before you, are most of them sad ones, though at the same time helpful; and because also I believe that your kind Irish hearts will answer more gladly to the truthful expression of a personal feeling than to the exposition of an abstract principle, I will permit myself so much unreserved speaking of my own causes of regret, as may enable you to make just allowance for what, according to your sympathies, you will call either the bitterness, or the insight, of a mind which has surrendered its best hopes, and been foiled in its favourite aims.

I spent the ten strongest years of my life, (from twenty to thirty,) in endeavouring to show the excellence of the work of the man whom I believed, and rightly believed, to be the greatest painter of the schools of England since Reynolds. I had then perfect faith in the power of every great truth of beauty to prevail ultimately, and take its right place in usefulness and honour; and I strove to bring the painter's work into this due place, while the painter was yet alive. But he knew, better than I, the uselessness of talking about what people could not see for themselves. He always discouraged me scornfully, even when he thanked me—and he died before even the superficial effect of my work was visible. I went on, however, thinking I could at least be of use to the public, if not to him, in proving his power. My books got talked about a little. The prices of modern pictures, generally, rose, and I was beginning to take some pleasure in a sense of gradual victory, when, fortunately or unfortunately, an opportunity of perfect trial undeceived me at once, and for ever. The Trustees of the National Gallery commissioned me to arrange the Turner drawings there, and permitted me to prepare three hundred examples of his studies from nature, for exhibition at Kensington. At Kensington they were and are, placed for exhibition: but they are not exhibited, for the room in which they hang is always empty.

Well—this showed me at once, that those ten years of my life had been, in their chief purpose, lost. For that, I did not so much care; I had, at least, learned my own business thoroughly, and should be able, as I fondly supposed, after such a lesson, now to use my knowledge with better effect. But what I did care for, was the—to me frightful—discovery, that the most splendid genius in the arts might be permitted by Providence to labour and perish uselessly; that in the very fineness of it there might be something rendering it invisible to ordinary eyes; but, that with this strange excellence, faults might be mingled which would be as deadly as its virtues were vain; that the glory of it was perishable, as well as invisible, and the gift and grace of it might be to us, as snow in summer, and as rain in harvest.

That was the first mystery of life to me. But, while my best energy was given to the study of painting, I had put collateral effort, more prudent, if less enthusiastic, into that of architecture; and in this I could not complain of meeting with no sympathy. Among several personal reasons which caused me to desire that I might give this, my closing lecture on the subject of art here, in Ireland, one of the chief was, that in reading it, I should stand near the beautiful building,—the engineers' school of your college,—which was the first realization I had the joy to see, of the principles I had, until then, been endeavouring to teach, but which, alas, is now, to me, no more than the richly canopied monument of one of the most earnest souls that ever gave itself to the arts, and one of my truest and most loving friends, Benjamin Woodward. Nor was it here in Ireland only that I received the help of Irish sympathy and genius. When, to another friend, Sir Thomas Deane, with Mr. Woodward, was entrusted the building of the museum at Oxford, the best details of the work were executed by sculptors who had been born and trained here; and the first window of the façade of the building, in which was inaugurated the study of natural science in England, in true fellowship with literature, was carved from my design by an Irish sculptor.

You may perhaps think that no man ought to speak of disappointment, to whom, even in one branch of labour, so much success was granted. Had Mr. Woodward now been beside me, I had not so spoken; but his gentle and passionate spirit was cut off from the fulfilment of its purposes, and the work we did together is now become vain. It may not be so in future; but the architecture we endeavoured to introduce is inconsistent alike with the reckless luxury, the deforming mechanism, and the squalid misery of modern cities; among the formative fashions of the day, aided, especially in England, by ecclesiastical sentiment, it indeed obtained notoriety; and sometimes behind an engine furnace, or a railroad bank, you may detect the pathetic discord of its momentary grace, and, with toil, decipher its floral carvings choked with soot. I felt answerable to the schools I loved, only for their injury. I perceived that this new portion of my strength had also been spent in vain; and from amidst streets of iron, and palaces of crystal, shrank back at last to the carving of the mountain and colour of the flower.

And still I could tell of failure, and failure repeated, as years went on; but I have trespassed enough on your patience to show you, in part, the causes of my discouragement. Now let me more deliberately tell you its results. You know there is a tendency in the minds of many men, when they are heavily disappointed in the main purposes of their life, to feel, and perhaps in warning, perhaps in mockery, to declare, that life itself is a vanity. Because it has disappointed them, they think its nature is of disappointment always, or at best, of pleasure, that can be grasped in imagination only; that the cloud of it has no strength nor fire within; but is a painted cloud only, to be delighted in, yet despised. You know how beautifully Pope has expressed this particular phase of thought :—

" Meanwhile opinion gilds, with varying rays,
   These painted clouds that beautify our days.
   Each want of happiness by hope supplied,
   And each vacuity of sense, by pride.
   Hope builds as fast as Knowledge can destroy;
   In Folly's cup, still laughs the bubble joy.
   One pleasure past, another still we gain,
   And not a vanity is given in vain.'

But the effect of failure upon my own mind has been just the reverse of this. The more that my life disappointed me, the more solemn and wonderful it became to me. It seemed, contrarily to Pope's saying, that the vanity of it *was* indeed given in vain; but that there was something behind the veil of it, which was not vanity. It became to me not a painted cloud, but a terrible and impenetrable one: not a mirage, which vanished as I drew near, but a pillar of darkness, to which I was forbidden to draw near. For I saw that both my own failure, and such success in petty things as in its various triumph seemed to me worse than failure, came from the want of sufficiently earnest effort to understand the whole law and meaning of existence, and to bring it to noble and due end; as, on the other hand, I saw more and more clearly that all enduring success in the arts, or in any other occupation, had come from the ruling of lower purposes, not by a conviction of their nothingness, but by a solemn faith in the advancing power of human nature, or in the promise, however dimly apprehended, that the mortal part

of it would one day be swallowed up in immortality; and
that, indeed, the arts themselves never had reached any
vital strength or honour but in the effort to proclaim this
immortality, and in the service either of great and just
religion, or of some unselfish patriotism, and law of such
national life as must be the foundation of religion.
Nothing that I have ever said is more true or necessary—
nothing has been more misunderstood or misapplied—
than my strong assertion, that the arts can never be right
themselves, unless their motive is right. It is misunderstood this way: weak painters, who have never learned
their business, and cannot lay a true line, continually
come to me, crying out—"Look at this picture of mine;
it *must* be good, I had such a lovely motive. I have put
my whole heart into it, and taken years to think over its
treatment." Well, the only answer for these people is—
if one had the cruelty to make it—"Sir, you cannot think
over *any*thing any number of years,—you haven't the
head to do it; and though you had fine motives, strong
enough to make you burn yourself in a slow fire, if only
first you could paint a picture, you can't paint one, nor
half an inch of one; you haven't the hand to do it."

But, far more decisively we have to say to the men
who *do* know their business, or may know if they choose
—"Sir, you have this gift, and a mighty one; see that
you serve your nation faithfully with it. It is a greater
trust than ships and armies: you might cast *them* away,
if you were their captain, with less treason to your people

than in casting your own glorious power away, and serving the devil with it instead of men. Ships and armies you may replace if they are lost, but a great intellect, once abused, is a curse to the earth for ever.

This, then, I meant by saying that the arts must have noble motive. This also I said respecting them, that they never had prospered, nor could prosper, but when they had such true purpose, and were devoted to the proclamation of divine truth or law. And yet I saw also that they had always failed in this proclamation—that poetry, and sculpture, and painting, though only great when they strove to teach us something about the gods, never had taught us anything trustworthy about the gods, but had always betrayed their trust in the crisis of it, and, with their powers at the full reach, became ministers to pride and to lust. And I felt also, with increasing amazement, the unconquerable apathy in ourselves the hearers, no less than in these the teachers; and that, while the wisdom and rightness of every act and art of life could only be consistent with a right understanding of the ends of life, we were all plunged in a languid dream —our heart fat, and our eyes heavy, and our ears closed, lest the inspiration of hand or voice should reach us— lest we should see with our eyes, and understand with our hearts, and be healed.

This intense apathy in all of us is the first great mystery of life; it stands in the way of every perception, every virtue. There is no making ourselves feel enough astonishment at it.   That the occupations or pastimes of life should have no motive, is understandable ; but that life itself should have no motive—that we neither care to find out what it may lead to, nor to guard against its being for ever taken away from us—here is a mystery indeed.   For just suppose I were able to call at this moment to any one in this audience by name, and to tell him positively that I knew a large estate had been lately left to him on some curious conditions; but that, though I knew it was large, I did not know how large, nor even where it was—whether in the East Indies or the West, or in England, or at the Antipodes.   I only knew it was a vast estate, and that there was a chance of his losing it altogether if he did not soon find out on what terms it had been left to him.   Suppose I were able to say this positively to any single man in this audience, and he knew that I did not speak without warrant, do you think that he would rest content with that vague knowledge, if it were anywise possible to obtain more ?   Would he not give every energy to find some trace of the facts, and never rest till he had ascertained where this place was, and what it was like ?   And suppose he were a young man, and all he could discover by his best endeavour was, that the estate was never to be his at all, unless he persevered during certain years of probation in an orderly and industrious life ; but that, according to the circumspection of his conduct, the portion of the estate assigned to him would be greater or less, so that it literally depended on his behaviour from day to day whether he got ten thousand a-year, or thirty thousand a-year, or nothing whatever—would you not think it strange if the youth never troubled himself to satisfy the conditions in any way, nor even to know what was required of him, but lived exactly as he chose, and never inquired whether his chances of the estate were increasing or passing away. Well, you know that this is actually and literally so with the greater number of the educated persons now living in Christian countries. Certainly nearly every man and woman, in any company such as this, outwardly professes to believe—and a large number unquestionably think they believe—much more than this; not only that a quite unlimited estate is in prospect for them if they please the Holder of it, but that the infinite contrary of such a possession—an estate of perpetual misery, is in store for them if they displease this great Land-Holder, this great Heaven-Holder. And yet there is not one in a thousand of these human souls that cares to think, for ten minutes of the day, where this estate is, or how beautiful it is, or what kind of life they are to lead in it, or what kind of life they must lead to obtain it. You fancy that you care to know this: so little do you care that, probably, at this moment many of you are displeased with me for talking of the matter! You came to hear about the art of this world, not about the life of the next, and you are provoked with me for talking of what you can hear any Sunday in church. But do not be afraid.

I will tell you something before you go about pictures, and carvings, and pottery, and what else you would like better to hear of than the other world. Nay, perhaps you say we want you to talk of pictures and pottery, because we are sure that you know something of them, and you know nothing of the other world. Well—I don't. That is quite true. But the very strangeness and mystery of which I urge you to take notice is in this— that I do not, nor you either. Can you answer a single bold question unflinchingly about that other world—Are you sure there is a heaven? Sure there is a hell? Sure that men are dropping before your faces through the pavements of these streets into eternal fire, or sure that they are not? Sure that at your own death you are going to be delivered from all sorrow, to be endowed with all virtue, to be gifted with all felicity, and raised into perpetual companionship with a King, compared to whom the kings of the earth are as grasshoppers and the nations as the dust of His feet? Are you sure of this? or, if not sure, do any of us so much as care to make it sure? and, if not, how can anything that we do be right—how can anything we think be wise ; what honor can there be in the arts that amuse us, or what profit in the possessions that please.

Is not this a mystery of life ?

But farther, you may, perhaps, think it a beneficent ordinance for the generality of men that they do not, with earnestness or anxiety, dwell on such questions of the future; and that the business of the day could not be done if this kind of thought were taken by all of us for the morrow. Be it so: but at least we might anticipate that the greatest and wisest of us, who were evidently the appointed teachers of the rest, would set themselves apart to seek out whatever could be surely known of the future destinies of their race, and to teach this in no rhetorical or ambiguous manner, but in the plainest and most severely earnest words.

Now, the highest representatives of men who have thus endeavoured, during the Christian era, to search out these deep things, and relate them, are Dante and Milton. There are none who for earnestness of thought, for mastery of word, can be classed with these. I am not at present, mind you, speaking of persons set apart in any priestly or pastoral office, to deliver creeds to us, or doctrines; but of men who try to discover and set forth, as far as by human intellect is possible, the facts of the other world. Divines may perhaps teach us how to arrive there, but only these two poets have in any powerful manner striven to discover, or in any definite words professed to tell, what we shall see and become there, or how those upper and nether worlds are, and have been, inhabited.

And what have they told us? Milton's account of the most important event in his whole system of the universe, the fall of the angels, is evidently unbelievable to himself; and the more so, that it is wholly founded on, and in a great part spoiled and degraded from, Hesiod's account of

the decisive war of the younger gods with the Titans.   The
rest of his poem is a picturesque drama, in which every
artifice of invention is visibly and consciously employed,
not a single fact being for an instant conceived as tenable
by any living faith.   Dante's conception is far more intense, and, by himself, for the time, not to be escaped from;
it is indeed a vision, but a vision only, and that one of the
wildest that ever entranced a soul—a dream in which every
grotesque type or phantasy of heathen tradition is renewed
and adorned; and the destinies of the Christian Church,
under their most sacred symbols, become literally subordi-
nate to the praise, and are only to be understood by the
aid, of one dear Florentine maiden.

Do you know, as I strive more sternly with this strange
lethargy and trance in myself, and awake to the meaning
and power of life, it seems daily more amazing to me that
men such as these should dare to play with the most precious truths, (or the most deadly untruths,) by which the
whole human race listening to them could be informed, or
deceived;—all the world their audiences for ever, with
pleased ear and passionate heart;—and yet, to this sub-
missive infinitude of souls, and evermore succeeding and
succeeding multitude, hungry for bread of life, they do but
play upon sweetly modulated pipes; with pompous nomen-
clature adorn the councils of hell; touch a troubadour's
gnitar to the courses of the suns; and fill the openings of
eternity, before which prophets have veiled their faces, and
which angels desire to look into, with idle puppets of their

scholastic imagination, and melancholy lights of frantic faith, in their lost mortal love.

Is not this a mystery of life? But more. We have to remember that these two great teachers were both of them warped in their temper and thwarted in their search for truth. They were men of intellectual war, unable, through darkness of controversy, or stress of personal grief, to discern where their own ambition modified their utterances of the moral law; or their own agony mingled with their anger at its violation. But greater men than these have been—men, innocent hearted—too great for contest. Men, like Homer and Shakespeare, of so unrecognized personality, that it disappears in future ages, and becomes ghostly, like the tradition of a lost heathen god. Men, therefore, to whose unoffended, uncondemning sight, the whole of human nature reveals itself in a pathetic weakness, with which they will not strive, or in mournful and transitory strength, which they dare not praise. And all Pagan and Christian civilization thus becomes subject to them. It does not matter how little, or how much, any of us have read, either of Homer or Shakespeare: everything round us, in substance, or in thought, has been moulded by them. All Greek gentlemen were educated under Homer. All Roman gentlemen, by Greek literature. All Italian, and French, and English gentlemen, by Roman literature, and by its principles. Of the scope of Shakespeare, I will say only, that the intellectual measure of every man since born, in the domains of creative thought, may be assigned to him, according to the degree in which he has been taught by Shakespeare. Well, what do these two men, centres of mortal intelligence, deliver to us of conviction, respecting what it most behoves that intelligence to grasp. What is their hope; their crown of rejoicing? what manner of exhortation have they for us, or of rebuke? what lies next their own hearts, and dictates their undying words? Have they any peace to promise to our unrest—any redemption to our misery?

Take Homer first, and think if there is any sadder image of human fate than the great Homeric story. The main features in the character of Achilles are its intense desire of justice, and its tenderness of affection. And in that bitter song of the Iliad, this man, though aided continually by the wisest of the gods, and burning with the desire of justice in his heart, becomes yet, through ill-governed passion, the most unjust of men; and, full of the deepest tenderness in his heart, becomes yet, through ill-governed passion, the most cruel of men; intense alike in love and in friendship, he loses, first, his mistress, and then his friend; for the sake of the one he surrenders to death the armies of his own land; for the sake of the other, he surrenders all. Will a man lay down his life for his friend? Yea—even for his dead friend, this Achilles, though goddess-born, and goddess-taught, gives up his kingdom, his country, and his life—casts alike the innocent and guilty, with himself, into one gulf of slaughter, and dies at last by the hand of the basest of his adversaries. Is not this a mystery of life?

But what, then, is the message to us of our own poet, and searcher of hearts, after fifteen hundred years of Christian faith have been numbered over the graves of men? Are his words more cheerful than the heathen's—is his hope more near—his trust more sure—his reading of fate more happy? Ah, no! He differs from the heathen poet chiefly in this—that he recognizes, for deliverance, no gods nigh at hand; and that, by petty chance — by momentary folly — by broken message — by fool's tyranny—or traitor's snare, the strongest and most righteous are brought to their ruin, and perish without word of hope. With necessary truth of insight, he indeed ascribes the power and modesty of habitual devotion, to the gentle and the just. The death-bed of Katharine is bright with vision of angels; and the great soldier-king, standing by his few dead, acknowledges the presence of the hand, that can save alike, by many or by few. But from those, who with deepest spirit, meditate, and with deepest passion, mourn, there are no such words as these; nor in their hearts such consolations. Instead of the perpetual sense of the helpful presence of the Deity, which through all heathen tradition is the source of heroic strength, in battle, in exile, and in the valley of the shadow of death, we find only in the great Christian poet, the consciousness of a moral law, through which " the gods are just, and of our pleasant vices make instruments to scourge us ;" and of the resolved arbitration of the destinies, that conclude into precision of doom what we feebly and blindly began; and force us, when our indiscretion serves us, and our deepest plots do pall, to the confession, that "there's a divinity that shapes our ends, rough hew them how we will."

Is not this a mystery of life?

Now observe: about this human life that is to be, or that is, the wise religious men tell us nothing that we can trust; and the wise contemplative men, nothing that can give us peace. But there is yet a third class, to whom we may turn—the wise practical men. We have sat at the feet of the poets who sang of heaven, and they have told us their dreams. We have listened to the poets who sang of earth, and they have chanted to us dirges, and words of despair. But there is one class of men more :—men, not capable of vision, nor sensitive to sorrow, but firm of purpose—practised in business; learned in all that can be, by handling, known. Men, whose hearts and hopes are wholly in this present world, from whom, therefore, we may surely learn, at least, how, at present, conveniently to live in it. What will *they* say to us, or show us by example? These kings—these councillors—these statesmen and builders of kingdoms—these capitalists and men of business, who weigh the earth and the dust of it in a balance. They know the world, surely; and what is the mystery of life to us, is none to them. They can surely show us how to live, while we live, and to gather out of the present world what is best.

I think I can best tell you their answer, by telling you a dream I had once. For though I am no poet, I have dreams sometimes:—I dreamed I was at a child's May-day party, in which every means of entertainment had been provided for them, by a wise and kind host. It was in a stately house, with beautiful gardens attached to it; and the children had been set free in the rooms and gardens, with no care whatever but how to pass their afternoon rejoicingly. They did not, indeed, know much about what was to happen next day; and some of them, I thought, were a little frightened, because there was a chance of their being sent to a new school where there were examinations; but they kept the thoughts of that out of their heads as well as they could, and resolved to enjoy themselves. The house, I said, was in a beautiful garden, and in the garden were all kinds of flowers; sweet grassy banks for rest; and smooth lawns for play; and pleasant streams and woods; and rocky places for climbing. And the children were happy for a little while, but presently they separated themselves into parties; and then each party declared, it would have a piece of the garden for its own, and that none of the others should have anything to do with that piece. Next, they quarrelled violently, which pieces they would have; and at last the boys took up the thing practically, and fought in the flower-beds till there was hardly a flower left stand-

2

ing; there they trampled down each other's bits of the garden out of spite; and the girls cried till they could cry no more; and so they all lay down at last breathless in the ruin, and waited for the time when they were to be taken home in the evening. Meanwhile, the children in the house had been making themselves happy also in their manner. For them, there had been provided every kind of in-doors pleasure: there was music for them to dance to; and the library was open, with all manner of amusing books; and there was a museum, full of the most curious shells, and animals, and birds; and there was a workshop, with lathes and carpenter's tools, for the ingenious boys; and there were pretty fantastic dresses, for the girls to dress in; and there were microscopes and kaleidoscopes; and whatever toys a child could fancy; and a table, in the dining-room, loaded with everything nice to eat.

But, in the midst of all this, it struck two or three of the more practical children, that they would like some of the brass-headed nails that studded the chairs, and they set to work to pull them out. Presently, the others, who were reading or looking at shells, took a fancy to do the like; and, in a little while, all the children nearly were spraining their fingers, in pulling out brass-headed nails. With all that they could pull out, they were not satisfied; and then, everybody wanted some of somebody else's. And at last, the really practical and sensible ones declared, that nothing was of any real consequence, that afternoon, except to get plenty of brass-headed nails; and that the books, and the cakes, and the microscopes, were of no use at all in themselves, but only, if they could be exchanged for nail-heads. And, at last, they began to fight for nail-heads, as the others fought for the bits of garden. Only here and there, a despised one shrank away into a corner, and tried to get a little quiet with a book, in the midst of the noise; but all the practical ones thought of nothing else but counting nail-heads all the afternoon—even though they knew they would not be allowed to carry so much as one brass knob away with them. But no—it was—"who has most nails? I have a hundred, and you have fifty; or, I have a thousand and you have two. I must have as many as you before I leave the house, or I cannot possibly go home in peace." At last, they made so much noise that I awoke, and thought to myself, "what a false dream that is, of *children*." The child is the father of the man; and wiser. Children never do such foolish things. But men do.

But there is yet one last class of persons to be interrogated. The wise religious men we have asked in vain; the wise contemplative men, in vain; the wise worldly men, in vain. But there is another group yet. In the midst of this vanity of empty religion—of tragic contemplation—of wrathful and wretched ambition, and dispute for dust, there is yet one great group of persons, by whom all these disputers live—the persons who have determined, or have had it by a beneficent Providence determined for them, that they will do something useful; that whatever may be prepared for them hereafter, or happen to them here, they will, at least, deserve the food that God gives them by winning it honourably; and that, however fallen from the purity, or far from the peace of Eden, they will carry out the duty of human dominion, though they have lost its felicity; and dress and keep the wilderness, though they no more can dress or keep the garden.

These,—hewers of wood, and drawers of water—these, bent under burdens, or torn of scourges—these, that dig and weave—that plant and build; workers in wood, and in marble, and in iron—by whom all food, clothing, habitation, furniture, and means of delight, are produced, for themselves, and for all men beside; men, whose deeds are good, though their words may be few; men, whose lives are serviceable, be they never so short, and worthy of honour, be they never so humble;—from these surely, at least, we may receive some clear message of teaching: and pierce, for an instant, into the mystery of life, and of its arts.

Yes; from these, at last, we do receive a lesson. But I grieve to say, or rather—for that is the deeper truth of the matter—I rejoice to say—this message of theirs can only be received by joining them—not by thinking about them.

You sent for me to talk to you of art; and I have obeyed you in coming. But, the main thing I have to tell you is,—that art must not be talked about. The fact that there is talk about it at all, signifies that it is ill done, or cannot be done. No true painter ever speaks, or ever has spoken, much of his art. The greatest speak nothing. Even Reynolds is no exception, for he wrote of all that he could not himself do, and was utterly silent respecting all that he himself did.

The moment a man can really do his work, he becomes speechless about it. All words become idle to him—all theories.

Does a bird need to theorize about building its nest, or boast of it when built. All good work is essentially done that way—without hesitation, without difficulty, without boasting ; and in the doers of the best, there is an inner and involuntary power which approximates literally to the instinct of an animal—nay, I am certain that in the most perfect human artists, reason does not supersede instinct, but is added to an instinct as much more divine than that of the lower animals as the human body is more beautiful than theirs ; that a great singer sings not with less instinct than the nightingale, but with more—only more various, applicable, and governable ; that a great architect does not build with less instinct than the beaver or the bee, but with more—with an innate cunning of proportion that embraces all beauty, and a divine ingenuity of skill that improvises all construction. But be that as it may—be the instinct less or more than that of inferior animals—like or unlike theirs, still the human art is dependent on that first, and then upon an amount of practice, of science,—and of imagination disciplined by thought, which the true possessor of it knows to be incommunicable, and the true critic of it, inexplicable, except through long process of laborious years. That journey of life's conquest, in which hills over hills, and Alps on Alps arose, and sank, do you think you can make another climb it painlessly, by talking? Why you cannot even carry us up an Alp with talking. You can guide us up it, step by step, no otherwise—even so, best silently. You girls who have been among the hills know how the bad guide chatters and gesticulates, and it is "put your foot here," and "mind how you balance yourself there;" but the good guide walks on quietly, without a word, only with his eyes on you when need is, and his arm like an iron bar, if need be. In that slow way, also, art can be taught—if you have faith in your guide, and will let his arm be to you as an iron bar when need is. But in what teacher of art have you such faith? Certainly not in me; for, as I told you at first, I know well enough it is only because you think I can talk, not because you think I know my business, that you let me speak to you at all. If I were to tell you anything that seemed to you strange, you would not believe it, and yet it would only be in telling you strange things that I could be of use to you. I could be of great use to you—infinite use, with brief saying, if you would believe it; but you would not, just because the thing that would be of real use would go against the grain with you. You are all wild, for

instance, with admiration of Gustave Dorè. Well, suppose I were to tell you, in the strongest terms I could use,
that Gustave Dorè's art was bad—bad, not in weakness,
not in failure, but bad with dreadful power—the power of
the Furies and the Harpies mingled, enraging, and pollu-
ting; that, so long as you looked at it, no perception of
pure or beautiful art was possible for you. Suppose I
were to tell you that! What would be the use? Would
you look at Gustave Dorè less? Rather, more, I fancy.
On the other hand, I could soon put you into good
humour with me, if I chose. I know well enough what
you like, and how to praise it, to your better liking. I
could talk to you about moonlight, and twilight, and
spring flowers, and autumn leaves, and the Madonnas of
Raphael—how motherly! and the Sibyls of Michael An-
gelo—how majestic! and the Saints of Angelico—how
pious! and the Cherubs of Correggio—how delicious!
Old as I am, I could play you a tune on the harp yet,
that you would dance to. But neither you nor I should
be a bit the better or wiser; or, if we were, our increased
wisdom could be of no practical effect. For, indeed, the
arts, as regards teachableness, differ from the sciences also
in this, that their power is founded not merely on facts
which can be communicated, but on dispositions which
require to be created. Art is neither to be achieved by
effort of thinking, nor explained by accuracy of speaking.
It is the instinctive and necessary result of powers which
can only be developed through the mind of successive

generations, and which finally burst into life under social conditions as slow of growth as the faculties they regulate. Whole æras of mighty history are summed, and the passions of dead myriads are concentrated, in the existence of a noble art; and if that noble art were among us, we should feel it and rejoice, and not care to hear lectures on it ; and since it is not among us, be assured we have to go back to the root of it, or, at least, to the place where the stock of it is yet alive, and the branches began to die.

And now, may I have your pardon for pointing out, partly with reference to matters which are at this time of greater moment than the arts—that if we undertook such recession to the vital germ of national arts that have decayed, we should find a more singular arrest of their power in Ireland than in any other European country. For in the eighth century, Ireland possessed a school of illumination, in many of its qualities—apparently in all essential qualities of invention and refinement—quite without rival ; seeming as if it might have advanced to the highest triumphs in architecture and in painting. But there was one fatal flaw in its nature, by which it was stayed, and stayed with a conspicuousness of pause to which there is no parallel ; so that long ago, in tracing for the students of Kensington, the progress of European schools from infancy to strength, I chose for them, in a lecture since published, two characteristic examples of early art, of equal skill ; but in the one case, skill which was progressive—in the other, skill which was at pause ;

in the one case, it was work necessarily receptive of correction—hungry for correction—and in the other, work which inherently rejected correction. I chose for them a corrigible Eve, and an incorrigible Angel, and I grieve to say, that the incorrigible Angel was also an Irish Angel!

And the fatal difference lay wholly in this. In both pieces of art there was an equal falling short of the needs of fact; but the Lombardic Eve knew she was in the wrong, and the Irish Angel thought himself all right. The eager Lombardic sculptor, though firmly insisting on his childish idea, yet showed in the irregular broken touches of the features, and the imperfect struggle for softer lines in the form, a perception of beauty and law that he could not render; there was the strain of effort under conscious imperfection in every line. But the Irish missal painter had drawn his angel with no sense of failure, in happy complacency, and put red dots into the palms of each hand, and rounded the eyes into perfect circles, and, I regret to say, left the mouth out altogether, with perfect satisfaction to himself.

May I, without offence, ask you to consider whether this mode of arrest in ancient Irish art may not be indicative of points of character which even yet, in some measure, arrest your national power? I have seen much of Irish character, and have watched it closely, for I have also much loved it. And I think the form of failure to which it is most liable is this, that being generous-hearted, and wholly intending always to do right, it does not attend to the external laws of right, but thinks it must necessarily do right because it means to do so, and therefore does wrong without finding it out; and then when the consequences of its wrong come upon it, or upon others connected with it, it cannot conceive that the wrong is in any wise of its causing or of its doing, but flies into wrath, and a strange agony of desire for justice, as feeling itself wholly innocent, which leads it farther astray, until there is nothing that it is not capable of doing with a good conscience.

But mind, I do not mean to say that in past or present relations between Ireland and England you have been wrong, and we right. Far from that; I believe that in all great questions of principle, and in all details of administration of law, you have been usually right and we wrong, sometimes in misunderstanding you, sometimes in resolute iniquity to you. Nevertheless, in all disputes between states, though the strongest is nearly always mainly in the wrong, the weaker is often so in a minor degree; and I think we sometimes admit the possibility of our being in error, and you never do.

And now, returning to the broader question, what these arts and labours of life have to teach us of its mystery, this is the first of their lessons—that the more beautiful the art, the more it is essentially the work of people who feel themselves wrong—who are striving for the fulfilment of the law and the realization of a loveliness which they have not yet attained, which they feel even farther and farther from attaining, the more they strive for it. And yet, in still deeper sense, it is the work of people who know also that they are right—and that this very sense of inevitable error from their purpose marks the perfectness of that purpose, and the manifold sense of failure arises from the opening of the eyes more clearly to all the sacredest laws of truth.

This is one lesson. The second, is a very plain, and greatly precious one, namely :—that whenever the arts and labours of life are fulfilled in this spirit of striving against misrule, and doing whatever we have to do, honourably and perfectly, they invariably bring happiness, as much as seems possible to the nature of man. In all other paths, by which that happiness is pursued, there is disappointment, or destruction ; for ambition and for passion there is no rest—no fruition ; the fairest pleasures of youth perish in a darkness greater than their past light ; and the loftiest and purest love too often does but inflame the cloud of life with endless fire of pain. But, ascending from lowest to highest, through every scale of human industry, that industry worthily followed, gives peace. Ask the labourer in the field, at the forge, or in the mine ; ask the patient, delicate-fingered artisan, or the strong-armed, fiery-hearted worker in bronze, and in marble, and with the colours of light ; and none of these, who are true workmen, will ever tell you, that they have found the law of heaven an unkind one—that in the sweat of their face they should eat bread, till they return to the ground; nor that they ever found it an unrewarded obedience, if, indeed, it was rendered faithfully to the command—"Whatsoever thy hand findeth to do—do it with thy might."

These are the two great and constant lessons which our labourers teach us of the mystery of life. But, there is another, and a sadder one, which they cannot teach us, which we must read on their tombstones.

"Do it with thy might." There have been myriads upon myriads of human creatures who have obeyed this law—who have put every breath and nerve of their being into its toil—who have devoted every hour, and exhausted every faculty—who have bequeathed their unaccomplished thoughts at death—who being dead, have yet spoken, by majesty of memory, and strength of example. And, at last, what has all this might of humanity accomplished, in six thousand years of labour and sorrow? What has it *done?* Take the three chief occupations and arts of men, one by one, and count their achievements. Begin with the first—the lord of them all—agriculture. Six thousand years have passed since we were set to till the ground, from which we were taken. How much of it is tilled? How much of that which is, wisely or well? Why, in the very centre and chief garden of Europe—where the two forms of parent Christianity have had their fortresses—where the noble Catholics of the Forest Cantons, and the noble Protestants of the Vaudois valleys, have maintained, for dateless ages, their faiths and liberties—there the un-

checked Alpine rivers yet run wild in devastation; and
the marshes, which a few hundred men could redeem with
a year's labour, still blast their helpless inhabitants into
fevered idiotism.   That is so, in the centre of Europe!
While, on the near coast of Africa, once the Garden of
the Hesperides, an Arab woman, but a few sunsets since,
ate her child, for famine.   And, with all the treasures of
the East at our feet, we, in our own dominion, could not
find a few grains of rice, for a people that asked of us no
more; but stood by, and saw five hundred thousand of
them perish of hunger.

Then, after agriculture, the art of kings, takes the next
head of human arts—weaving, the art of queens, honoured
of all noble Heathen women, in the person of their virgin
goddess—honoured of all Hebrew women, by the word of
their wisest king—" She layeth her hands to the spindle,
and her hands hold the distaff; she stretcheth out her
hand to the poor.   She is not afraid of the snow for her
household, for all her household are clothed with scarlet.
She maketh herself covering of tapestry; her clothing is
silk and purple.   She maketh fine linen, and selleth it,
and delivereth girdles to the merchant."   What have we
done in all these thousands of years with this bright art
of Greek maid and Christian matron?   Six thousand years
of weaving, and have we learned to weave?   Might not
every naked wall have been purple with tapestry, and
every feeble breast fenced with sweet colours from the
cold?   What have we done?   Our fingers are too few, it

seems, to twist together some poor covering for our bodies. We set our streams to work for us, and choke the air with fire, to turn our spinning-wheels—and, are we yet clothed? Are not the streets of the capitals of Europe foul with sale of cast clouts and rotten rags. Is not the beauty of your sweet children left in wretchedness of disgrace, while, with better honour, nature clothes the brood of the bird in its nest, and the suckling of the wolf in her den. And does not every winter's snow robe what you have not robed, and shroud what you have not shrouded; and every winter's wind bear up to heaven its wasted souls, to witness against you hereafter, by the voice of their Christ.—" I was naked, and ye clothed me not."

Lastly — take the Art of Building — the strongest — proudest—most orderly—most enduring, of the arts of man ; that, of which the produce is in the surest manner accumulative, and need not perish, or be replaced ; but if once well done, will stand more strongly than the unbalanced rocks—more prevalently than the crumbling hills. The art which is associated with all civic pride and sacred principle ; in which men record their power—satisfy their enthusiasm—make sure their defence—define and make dear their habitations. And, in six thousand years of building, what have we done? Of the greater part of all that skill and strength, *no* vestige is left, but fallen stones, that encumber the fields and impede the streams. But, from this waste of disorder, and of time, and of rage, what *is* left to us? Constructive and progressive creatures, that we are, with ruling brains, and forming hands, capable of fellowship, and thirsting for fame, can we not contend, in comfort, with the insects of the forest, or, in achievement, with the worm of the sea. The white surf rages in vain against the ramparts built by poor atoms of scarcely nascent life, but only ridges of formless ruin mark the places where once dwelt our noblest multitudes. The ant and the moth have cells for each of their young, but our little ones lie in festering heaps, in homes that consume them like graves; and night by night, from the corners of our streets, rises up the cry of the homeless—"I was a stranger, and ye took me not in."

Must it be always thus? Is our life for ever to be without profit—without possession? Shall the strength of its generations be as barren as death; or cast away their labour, as the wild figtree casts her untimely figs? Is it all a dream then—the desire of the eyes and the pride of life—or, if it be, might we not live in nobler dreams than these? The poets and prophets, the wise men, and the scribes, though they have told us nothing about a life to come, have told us much about the life that is now. They have had—they also,—their dreams, and we have laughed at them. They have dreamed of mercy, and of justice; they have dreamed of peace and good-will; they have dreamed of labour undisappointed, and of rest undisturbed; they have dreamed of fulness in harvest, and overflowing in store; they have dreamed of wisdom in council, and of providence in law; of gladness of parents, and strength of children, and glory of gray hairs. And at these visions of theirs we have mocked, and held them for idle and vain, unreal and unaccomplishable. What have we accomplished with our realities? Is this what has come of our worldly wisdom, tried against their folly? this, our mightiest possible, against their impotent ideal? or, have we only wandered among the spectra of a baser felicity, and chased phantoms of the tombs, instead of visions of the Almighty; and walked after the imaginations of our evil hearts, instead of after the counsels of Eternity, until our lives—not in the likeness of the cloud of heaven, but of the smoke of hell— have become "even as a vapour, that appeareth for a little time, and then vanisheth away"?

Does it vanish then? Are you sure of that?—sure that the nothingness of the grave will be a rest from this troubled nothingness; and that the coiled shadow, which disquieteth itself in vain, cannot change into the smoke of the torment that ascends for ever? Will any answer that they *are* sure of it, and that there is no fear, nor hope, nor desire, nor labour, whither they go? Be it so; will you not, then, make as sure of the life that now is, as you are of the death that is to come? Your hearts are wholly in this world—will you not give them to it wisely, as well as perfectly? And see, first of all, that you *have* hearts, and sound hearts, too, to give. Because you have no heaven to look for, is that any reason that you should remain ignorant of this wonderful and infinite earth, which is surely and instantly given you in possession? Although your days are numbered, and the following darkness sure, is it necessary that you should share the degradation of the brute, because you are condemned to its mortality; or live the life of the moth, and of the worm, because you are to companion with them in the dust? Not so; we may have but a few thousand of days to spend, perhaps hundreds only—perhaps, tens; nay, the longest of our time and best, looked back on, will be but as a moment, as the twinkling of an eye; but yet, we are men, not insects; we are living spirits, not passing clouds. He maketh the winds his angels; the flaming fire, his ministers. And shall we do less than these? Let us do the work of men while we bear the form of them, and as we snatch our narrow portion of time out of Eternity, snatch also our narrow but glorious inheritance of passion out of Immortality—even though our lives be as a vapour, that appeareth for a little time, and then vanisheth away.

But there are some of you who believe not this—who think this cloud of life has no such close—that it is to float, revealed and illumined, upon the floor of heaven in the day when He cometh with clouds, and every eye shall see Him. Some day, you believe, within these five or ten or twenty years, for every one of us the judgment will be set, and the books opened. If that be true, far more than that must be true. Is there but one day of judgment? Why, for us every day is a day of judgment

—every day is a **Dies Iræ,** and writes its irrevocable verdict in the flame of the west. Think you that judgment waits till the doors of the grave are opened. It waits at the doors of your houses—it waits at the corners of your streets; we are in the midst of judgment—the creatures whom we crush are our judges—the moments we fret away are our judges—the elements that feed us judge as they minister—and the pleasures that deceive us judge as they indulge. Let *us*, for our lives, do the work of **Men** while we bear the **Form** of them, since those lives are *Not* as a vapour, and do Not vanish away.

"The work of men"—and what is that? Well, we may any of us know it very quickly, on the condition of being wholly ready to do it. But many of us are for the most part thinking, not of what we are to do, but of what we are to get; and the best of us are sunk into the sin of Ananias, and it is a mortal one—we want to keep back part of the price; and we continually talk of taking·up our cross, as if the only mischief in a cross was the weight of it—as if it was only a thing to be carried, instead of to be crucified upon. "They that are His have crucified the flesh, with the affections and lusts." Does that mean, think you, that in time of national distress, of religious trial, of crisis for every interest and hope of humanity— none of us will cease jesting, none cease idling, none put themselves to any wholesome work, none take so much as a tog of lace off their footman's coats, to save the world? Or does it rather mean, that they are ready to leave houses, lands, and kindreds—yes, and life, if need be? Life!—some of us are ready enough to throw that away, joyless as we have made it. But " station in Life "—how many of us are ready to quit that? Is it not always the great objection, where there is question of finding something useful to do—" We cannot leave our stations in Life?"

Now, those of us who really cannot—that is to say, who can only maintain themselves by continuing in some business or salaried office, have already something to do; and all that they have to see to, is that they do it honestly and with all their might. But with most people who use that apology, "remaining in the station of life to which Providence has called them," means keeping all the carriages, and all the footmen and large houses they can possibly pay for; and, once for all, I say that if ever Providence put them into stations of that sort—which is not at all a matter of certainty—Providence is just now very distinctly calling them out again. Levi's station in life was the receipt of Custom, and Peter's the shore of Galilee, and Paul's the antechambers of the High Priest, which "station in life " each had to leave with brief notice.

And, whatever our station in life may be, at this crisis, those of us who mean to fulfil our duty ought first, to live on as little as we can; and secondly, to do all the wholesome work for it we can, and to spend all we can spare in doing all the sure good we can.

And sure good is first in feeding people, then in dressing

people, then in lodging people, and lastly in rightly pleasing people, with arts, or sciences, or any other subject of thought.

I say first in feeding; and, once for all, do not let yourselves be deceived by any of the common talk of indiscriminate charity. The order to us is not to feed the deserving hungry, nor the industrious hungry, nor the amiable and well-intentioned hungry, but simply to feed the hungry. It is quite true, infallibly true, that if any man will not work, neither should he eat—think of that, and every time you sit down to your dinner, ladies and gentlemen, say solemnly, before you ask a blessing, "How much work have I done to-day for my dinner"—but the proper way to enforce that order on those below you, as well as on yourselves, is not to leave vagabonds and honest people to starve together, but very distinctly to discern and seize your vagabond, and shut your vagabond up out of honest people's way, and very sternly then see that, until he has worked, he does *not* eat. But the first thing is to be sure you have the food to give; and, therefore, the organization of vast activities in agriculture and in commerce, for the production of the wholesomest food, and proper storing and distribution of it, so that no famine shall any more be possible among civilized beings. There is plenty of work in this business alone, and at once, for any number of people who like to engage in it.

Secondly, dressing people—that is to say, urging every-one within reach of your influence to be always neat and clean, and giving them means of being so. In so far as they absolutely refuse, you must give up the effort with respect to them, only taking care that no children within your sphere of influence shall any more be brought up with such habits, and that every person who is willing to dress with propriety shall have encouragement in doing so. And the first absolutely necessary step towards this is the gradual adoption of a consistent dress for different ranks of persons, so that their rank shall be known by their dress; and the restriction of the changes of fashion within certain limits. All which appears for the present quite impossible; but it is only so far as even difficult as it is difficult to conquer our vanity, frivolity, and desire to appear what we are not.

And it is not, nor ever shall be, creed of mine, that these mean and shallow vices are unconquerable by Christian women.

And then, thirdly, lodging people, which you may think should have been put first, but I put it third, because we must feed and clothe people where we find them, and lodge them afterwards. And providing lodgment for them means a great deal of vigorous legislation, and cutting down of vested interests that stand in the way, and after that, or before that, so far as we can get it, thorough sanitary and remedial action in the houses that we have; and then the building of more, strongly and beautifully, but in groups of limited extent, kept in proportion to their streams, and walled round, so that there might be no fes-

tering and wretched suburb anywhere, but clean and busy
street here, and the open country there, with a belt of
beautiful garden and orchard round the walls, so that from
any part of the city perfectly fresh air and grass, and sight
of far horizon might be reachable in a few minutes' walk.
This the final aim; but in immediate action every minor and
possible good to be instantly done, when and as we can;
roofs mended that have holes in them—fences that have
gaps in them—walls that totter—and floors that shake;
cleanliness and order enforced with our own hands and
eyes, till we are breathless, every day. And all the fine
arts will healthily follow. I myself have washed a flight
of stone stairs all down, with bucket and broom, in a Savoy
inn, where they hadn't washed their stairs since they first
went up them, and I never made a better sketch than that
afternoon.

These, then, are the three needs of civilized life; and the
law for every Christian man and woman is, that they shall
be in direct service towards one of these three needs, as
far as is consistent with their own special occupation, and
if they have no special business, then wholly in one of these
services. And out of such exertion in plain duty all other
good will come; for in this direct contention with material
evil, you will find out the real nature of all evil; you will
discern by the various kinds of resistance, what is really
the fault and main antagonism to good; also you will find
the most unexpected helps and profound lessons given, and
truths will come thus down to us which the speculation of

all our lives would never have raised us up to. You will find nearly every educational problem solved, as soon as you truly want to do something; everybody will become of use in their own fittest way, and will learn what is best for them to know in that use. Competitive examination will then, and not till then, be wholesome, because it will be daily, and calm, and in practice; and on these familiar arts, and minute, but certain and serviceable, knowledges, will be surely edified and sustained, the greater arts and splendid theoretical sciences.

But much more than this. On such holy and simple practice will be founded, indeed, at last, an infallible religion. The greatest of all the mysteries of life and the most terrible, is the corruption of even the sincerest religion, which is not daily founded on rational, effective, humble, and helpful action. Helpful action, observe! for there is just one law, which obeyed, keeps all religions pure—forgotten, makes them all false. Whenever in any religious faith, dark or bright, we allow our minds to dwell upon the points in which we differ from other people, we are wrong, and in the devil's power. That is the essence of the Pharisee's thanksgiving—"Lord, I thank thee that I am not as other men are." At every moment of our lives we should be trying to find out, not in what we differ with other people, but in what we agree with them; and the moment we find we can agree as to anything that should be done, kind or good, (and who but fools couldn't?) then do it; push at it together; you can't quarrel in a side-by-

side push; but the moment that even the best men stop
pushing, and begin talking, they mistake their pugnacity
for piety, and it's all over. I will not speak of the crimes
which in past times have been committed in the name of
Christ, nor of the follies which are at this hour held to be
consistent with obedience to Him ; but I will speak of the
morbid corruption and waste of vital power in religious
sentiment, by which the pure strength of that which should
be the guiding soul of every nation, the splendour of its
youthful manhood, and spotless light of its maidenhood, is
averted or cast away. You may see continually girls who
have never been taught to do a single useful thing thoroughly ; who cannot sew, who cannot cook, who cannot
cast an account, nor prepare a medicine, whose whole life
has been passed either in play or in pride ; you will find
girls like these, when they are earnest-hearted, cast all
their innate passion of religious spirit, which was meant
by God to support them through the irksomeness of daily
toil, into grievous and vain meditation over the meaning
of the great Book, of which no syllable was ever yet to be
understood but through a deed; all the instinctive wisdom
and mercy of their womanhood made vain, and the glory
of their pure consciences warped into fruitless agony con-
cerning questions which the laws of common serviceable
life would have either solved for them in an instant, or
kept out of their way. Give such a girl any true work
that will make her active in the dawn, and weary at night,
with the consciousness that her fellow-creatures have in-

deed been the better for her day, and the powerless sorrow of her enthusiasm will transform itself into a majesty of radiant and beneficent peace.

So with our youths. We once taught them to make Latin verses, and called them educated; now we teach them to leap and to row, and to hit a ball with a bat, and call them educated. Can they plough, can they sow, can they plant at the right time, or build with a steady hand? Is it the effort of their lives to be chaste, knightly, faithful, holy in thought, lovely in word and deed? Indeed it is, with some, nay with many, and the strength of England is in them, and the hope; but we have to turn their courage from the toil of war to the toil of mercy; and their intellect from dispute of words to discernment of things; and their knighthood from the errantry of adventure to the state and fidelity of a kingly power. And then, indeed, shall abide for them and for us an incorruptible felicity, and an infallible religion; shall abide for us Faith, no more to be assailed by temptation, no more to be defended by wrath and by fear;—shall abide with us Hope, no more to be quenched by the years that overwhelm, or made ashamed by the shadows that betray;—shall abide for us, and with us, the greatest of these—the abiding will—the abiding name of our Father—for the greatest of these is Charity.